This book belongs to

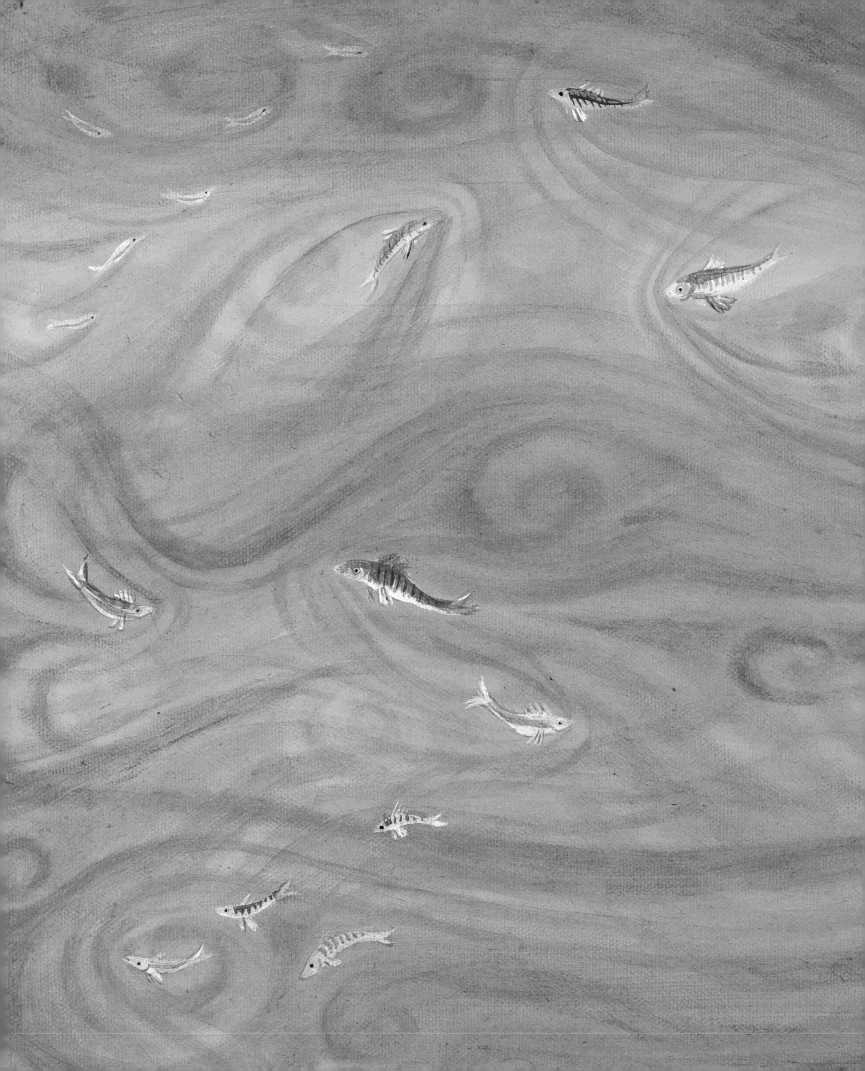

This edition published by Parragon in 2011

Parragon
Queen Street House
4 Queen Street
Bath BA1 1HE, UK

ISBN 978-1-4454-3462-9

Printed in China

Just One More Swim

Caroline Pitcher and Jenny Jones

PaRragon

Bath · New York · Singapore · Hong Kong · Cologne · Delhi
Melbourne · Amsterdam · Johannesburg · Auckland · Shenzhen

Big Bear's tiny cubs were safe inside her snowdrift den. The cubs woke up. They yawned and stretched. They turned their heads toward the sound of the ocean.

Big Bear stood up and sniffed the air.
She lumbered out toward the water.
The cubs scampered after her,
blinking at the dazzling world.

Big Bear padded across the ice.
She stopped and dug a hole.
She dipped in her paw and scooped out…

…a fish!

The cubs did just what Big Bear did.

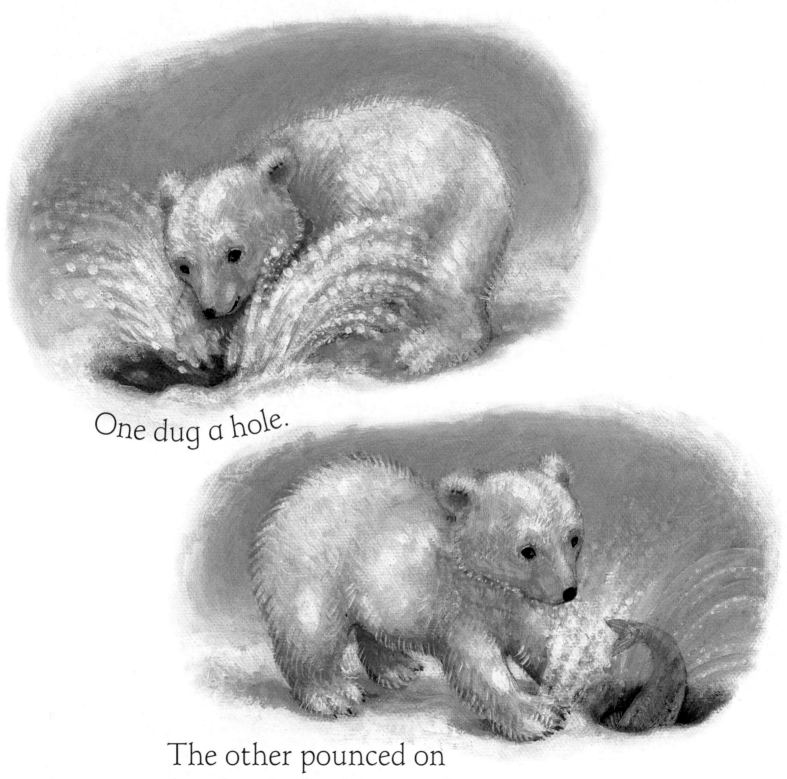

One dug a hole.

The other pounced on
the cloud of white, and
frightened off the fish.

The cubs squabbled. They fought.
They tackled each other
and tumbled and rolled,
over and over in
the snow.

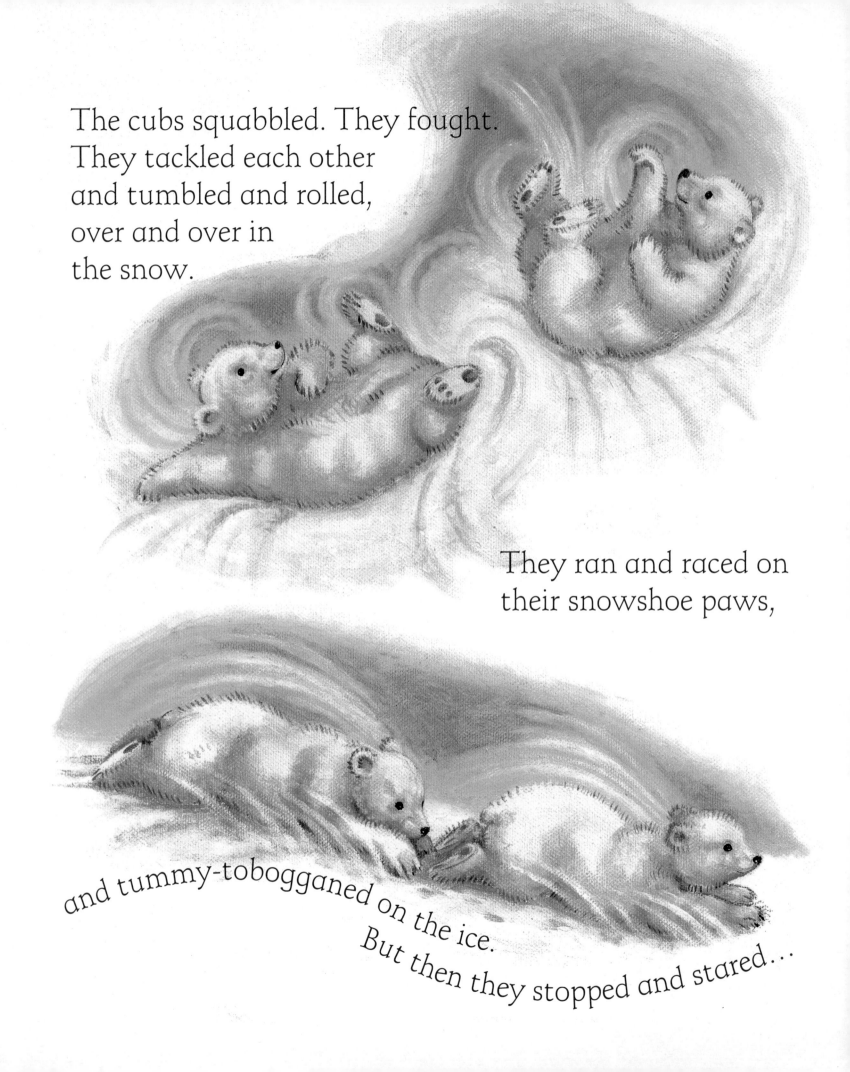

They ran and raced on
their snowshoe paws,

and tummy-tobogganed on the ice.
But then they stopped and stared...

"What is that?" they asked.
The cubs trembled as they gazed at
the blue-green water ahead.

Every morning, Big Bear
coaxed her cubs a little
further toward the ocean.

Then one day, Big Bear and her cubs slowly and
carefully made their way to the water's edge.
Big Bear gently slid into the icy sea.
The cubs jumped up and squealed.
"Come back!" they cried.

But Big Bear swam out strongly to an
island of ice in the waves.

The cubs waited for her,
shivering on the thin ice.
They watched seals curve over
the rolling waves, and saw
silver fish flip and spin.

The water rippled. The cubs patted it—
but it just wouldn't stay still.
Then they put two paws in…and pulled
them right back out again.

Big Bear called to her cubs to swim over to the island.
"Come to me across the ocean," she urged.
Up in the air the seabirds flew, crying "Swim! Swim!"
"You can do it," called Big Bear. "I know you can."

"Swim!"

"Swim!"

And they did!

Before they knew it, the cubs were swimming too. Under the water they went, twisting and turning in the aquamarine sea.

Up to the top of the water they swam, passing a narwhal with his sword and a whiskered walrus too. Then they dived down from on high, cutting through the waves.

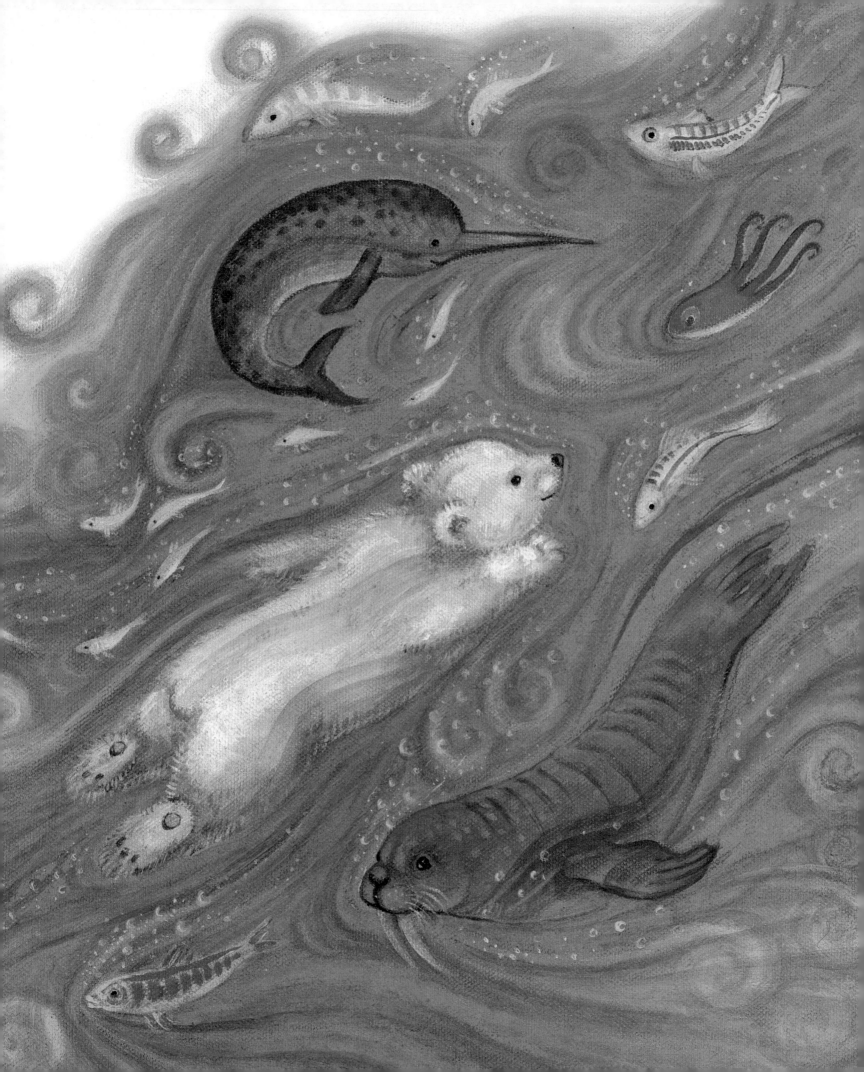

The cubs paddled with their powerful paws,
over and under the Arctic waves.
They splashed and thrashed and somersaulted
through the icy water.

"So this is what we do!"

"We can swim too!"

They paddled and swam until
Big Bear insisted, "Come out now!"
The cubs pulled their weary bodies onto the ice,
shaking rainbow drops all over Big Bear.

Then Big Bear led her cubs to
where the juicy blueberries grow.
The cubs ate and ate, until their
muzzles and paws turned blue.

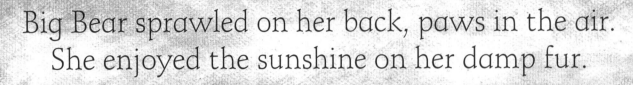

Big Bear sprawled on her back, paws in the air.
She enjoyed the sunshine on her damp fur.

But the cubs had other ideas. And, as they headed
back toward the water one more time,
Big Bear smiled as she heard their call…

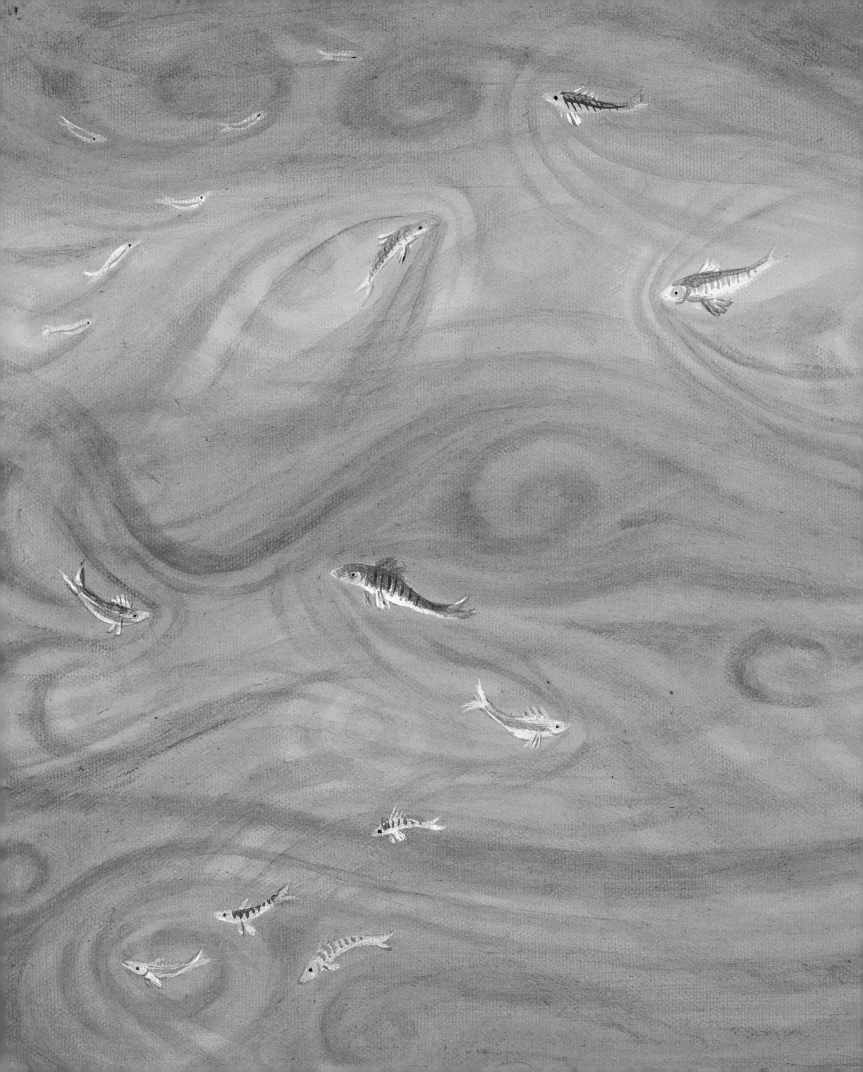